THE
LITTLE REINDEER

For Jay, Jean, Marion, and the original
reindeer girls, Rosie and Raffi

SIMON & SCHUSTER BOOKS FOR YOUNG READERS
An imprint of Simon & Schuster Children's Publishing Division
1230 Avenue of the Americas, New York, New York 10020
Text and illustrations copyright © 2016 by Nicola Killen
Originally published in Great Britain in 2016 by Simon & Schuster UK Ltd.
Published by arrangement with Simon & Schuster UK Ltd.
First US edition 2017
All rights reserved, including the right of reproduction in whole or in part in any form.
SIMON & SCHUSTER BOOKS FOR YOUNG READERS is a trademark of Simon & Schuster, Inc.
For information about special discounts for bulk purchases, please contact Simon & Schuster
Special Sales at 1-866-506-1949 or business@simonandschuster.com.
The Simon & Schuster Speakers Bureau can bring authors to your live event.
For more information or to book an event, contact the Simon & Schuster Speakers
Bureau at 1-866-248-3049 or visit our website at www.simonspeakers.com.
The text for this book was set in Corda.
Manufactured in China
0816 SUK
10 9 8 7 6 5 4 3 2 1
CIP data for this book is available from the Library of Congress.
ISBN 978-1-4814-8686-6
ISBN 978-1-4814-8687-3 (eBook)

THE
LITTLE REINDEER

Nicola Killen

A Paula Wiseman Book
Simon & Schuster Books for Young Readers
New York   London   Toronto   Sydney   New Delhi

It was Christmas Eve and Ollie had just gone to sleep when

jingle, jingle, jingle

she woke again with a start.

What was that sound?

She rushed to the window, but all she could see was a blanket of fresh snow!

Grabbing her sled, she ran downstairs...

and stepped out into
the wintry night.

Ollie jumped up to catch a falling snowflake,
when she heard the magical sound again.

Jingle, jingle, jingle.

She had to follow it.

Whoooooooosh!

Racing down the hill, she heard the ringing again.

Jingle, jingle, jingle.

And this time it was much clearer.

The bells got louder as the wind
whistled and the trees shook.

Jingle, jingle, jingle.

Ollie was getting close.

There, hanging from a branch,
was a collar circled with silver bells.

Who could it belong to?

Then came a new sound . . .

She took a deep breath and, feeling very brave, she ran into the darkness.

Crunch, crunch, crunch.

A reindeer stepped through the crisp snow toward Ollie.

"H...h...hello," she whispered, not quite believing her eyes. "Are you looking for this?"

The reindeer knelt down patiently while Ollie fastened his collar.
Then he lowered himself even farther.

Ollie knew exactly what to do and climbed onto his back.
She wondered if they would go for a ride through the forest,
but to her surprise . . .

they soared up into the night sky,
leaving the trees far below!

The new friends landed softly in the snow. "Thank you," Ollie whispered.

They didn't want to part, but there was someone very special who needed the reindeer's help that night.

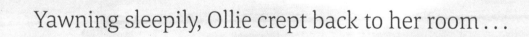
Yawning sleepily, Ollie crept back to her room . . .

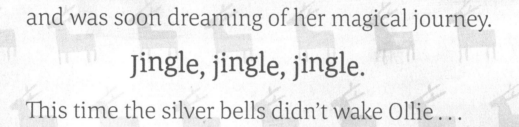

and was soon dreaming of her magical journey.

Jingle, jingle, jingle.

This time the silver bells didn't wake Ollie...

as her reindeer flew
through the night sky
once more.

In the morning, Ollie found her presents.
Now she would always think of her new friend.
"See you next year!" she whispered.